Sir
Lilypad

SIMON AND SCHUSTER

First published in Great Britain in 2015 by Simon and Schuster UK Ltd
1st Floor, 222 Gray's Inn Road, London WC1X 8HB
A CBS Company

Text copyright © 2015 Anna Kemp
Illustrations copyright © 2015 Sara Ogilvie

A CIP catalogue record for this book is available from the British Library upon request

ISBN: 978-0-85707-514-7 (HB) · ISBN: 978-0-85707-515-4 (PB)
ISBN: 978-1-4711-2363-4 (eBook)
Printed in China   10 9 8 7 6 5 4 3 2 1

For Kyle and Matthe
- SO

For my dear nephew
Joseph, aka 'Frogger'
- AK

Sir Lilypad

a tall tale of a small frog

Anna Kemp and Sara Ogilvie

SIMON AND SCHUSTER
London   New York   Sydney   Toronto   New Delhi

Once upon a time, in a deep dark bog,
Lived a teeny-tiny speckled frog.
His brothers called him Little Tad
But he preferred –

Sir Lilypad!

Sir Lilypad the proud and free!
A knight in slimy armour he!
Sir Lilypad the brave and wise!
Slayer of the dragonflies.

But no one takes you seriously,
When you're not much bigger than a pea.

And so Sir Lily wished and longed
To grow up big and tall and strong.

Then, one night, tucked in his nook
He read the most terrific book!
Frog to prince with one small kiss
From a grateful royal miss.

Sir Lily scratched his speckled head.
"I'd never thought of that," he said.
"If I could save a princess true,
I'd surely grow a foot or two!"

Next morning, feeling tough and brave, he hopped off to the local cave.

And found an ogre, vast and green . . .

A-watering his runner beans.
"Halt, foul ogre! Where's the dame?"
Croaked Sir Lily, eyes aflame.

The ogre shook his massive head.
"I'm far too old for that," he said.
"And you're too small, don't you agree,
For bashing giant-folk like me?
You should be getting home, my dear.
Does your mummy know you're here?"

Sir Lily blushed from tip to toe.
But was he beaten? Heavens, no!

And so he searched the bolted towers . . .

. . . the forest

and the field of flowers.

The witch's house

and
wizard's
tree . . .

But every one was princess-free!

By now Sir Lily had a stitch.

His chainmail pants began to itch.

His sandwiches were getting soggy.
Oh, what a wretched little froggy!

But wait a sec! What's over there?

A sudden glimpse of flowing hair!
Sparkling eyes and cherry lips –

a broadsword slung around the hips.

Still, nevermind, a fair princess!
And in a dragon's grip no less!

Sir Lily gave a mighty croak
And charged right through the dragon's smoke.
"Release that maiden fair!" he roared.
Then poked him with his wooden sword.

"I say," said Dragon. "Do you mind?
It's rude to creep up from behind."

But Sir Lily, undeterred,
Pretended that he hadn't heard.

"Now flee back to your darkened den!
Or else I'll poke you once again!"

"Slow down, froggy!" laughed the lady.
"That's my friend! No need to save me!
And have you seen me in a fight?
I just don't need a noble knight."

Brave Sir Lily turned quite pale
Then suddenly began to

Wail!

"But now I'll be forever small!
And not a proper knight at all.

The other frogs will call me stuff
Like weedy-pants and sugar-puff.
I'll always just be tiny Tad
And never Brave Sir Lilypad!"

The princess shook her head and laughed.
"But Lilypad, you're being daft.
Froglets can be heroes too.
Why don't you join our motley crew?"

"Can I? Really?" Lily blinked.

"You betcha, froggy," Princess winked.

"Arise, Sir Lilypad the Green!
Bravest frog we've ever seen!"

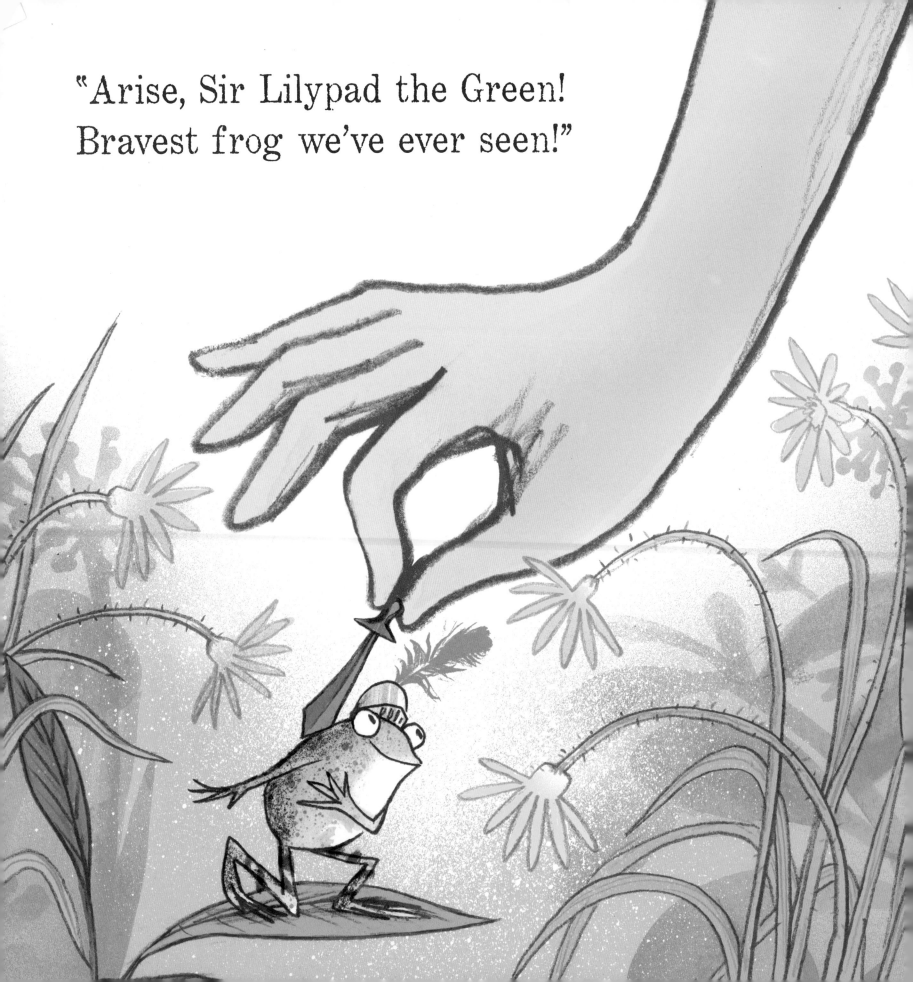

From that day on our fearless knight
Forgot his under-average height.
He sought adventure, joined the fray –

and poked some baddies on the way!

He cut the bullies down to size,
Stood up for all the little guys.

Till news spread far across the land
Of Lily and his gallant band.

And centuries later, tales were read
To wide-eyed tadpoles, tucked in bed,
Of all the great adventures had
By small, but brave, Sir Lilypad.